Wild Song

by

Jane Eagland

For Sheila

First American edition published in 2013 by Stoke Books,
an imprint of Barrington Stoke Ltd

18 Walker Street, Edinburgh, United Kingdom, EH3 7LP

www.stokebooks.com

A catalog record for this book is available from
the US Library of Congress

Distributed in the United States and Canada by Lerner Publisher
Services, a division of Lerner Publishing Group, Inc.

241 First Avenue North, Minneapolis, MN 55401

www.lernerbooks.com.

ISBN 978-1-78112-182-5

Printed in China

Contents

Chapter 1

The Storm

Anna stood as close to the cliff top as she dared, gazing out to sea.

The angry wind whipped loose strands of her hair into her eyes. Below her the water crashed and foamed against the rocks and fountains of spray flew up into the air. Seabirds screamed overhead, white against the gray sky.

Anna shivered, more from fear than the cold.

Behind her, across the water, lay the mainland of Scotland. But she was out here, on this small rocky island. Again and again the sea threw itself against the land as if it were trying to swallow it up. It terrified her. But she couldn't tear herself away.

These wild days stirred her up. They made her feel wild herself. They made her feel there was something she wanted but she didn't know what it was.

She watched the dark wall of rain race towards her.

From behind her there came the sound of the castle bell. She knew it was calling for her. It was time to see her father.

But still she stayed, until the last minute. Until the first cold drops of rain fell on her face.

***

At the castle Biddy was waiting in the warm kitchen. She whisked off Anna's coat and hung it near the fire to dry.

"What were you thinking?" she scolded. "You'll catch a cold."

Anna took off her boots and put on her velvet slippers.

"Only my coat got wet," she said. "Look, my dress is dry." She spread her skirt wide as proof.

Biddy snorted and fetched a towel to dry Anna's long hair.

Sometimes Biddy's fussing got on Anna's nerves. But she was fond of her old nurse. Biddy told her stories even though she wasn't supposed to.

Now Biddy said, "Didn't you hear Jasper ringing the bell?"

Anna didn't answer. Biddy wouldn't understand about the wildness.

Just then, Jasper himself came through the kitchen. The smell of cow dung came with him.

Anna didn't like Biddy's husband much, even if she tried not to show it.

For one thing there was something wrong with his eyes. You never knew if he was looking at you or not. It was creepy.

She was glad she didn't have to see him very often. He did the heavy work on the island, and looked after the crops and the animals.

Now he nodded at Anna and his wife and went into the room where he and Biddy slept. Unlike Biddy, he never had much to say for himself.

At last Biddy was happy. She tucked a shawl around Anna's shoulders and gave her a little push. "Go on now. Your father's waiting."

***

Anna left the kitchen and crossed the shadowy Great Hall. The rain beat against its tall windows and the wind moaned in the chimney, like a trapped creature. Anna didn't notice. She was used to the sounds the castle made in bad weather.

She climbed the spiral staircase, up and up. At last she reached the room at the very top of the tower. Behind its closed door, her father, Lord Grey, spent most of his time.

She paused to smooth her hair, then knocked.

Max, her father's assistant opened the door. His real name was Mr. Maxwell but her father called him Max so she did too.

He greeted her, grave as always. "Ah, there you are, Miss Anna."

Anna smiled a shy smile as she went in.

It was funny. She'd known Max all her life. But in the last few months she'd started to think about him more. He was quite a bit older than her, probably in his thirties, she guessed. But he was tall and now she saw he was very good-looking. And when he looked right at her with those light blue eyes of his, she felt strange. A bit shivery, but in a nice way.

She saw him almost every day to go over assignments, but sometimes she wished they had time to talk about other things. She wondered if he felt the same. If he cared for her at all.

She thought he might. Over the last few years someone had been leaving books for her in her room. In secret. Books her father couldn't know about, because he wouldn't want her to read them. It had to be Max. No one else would do that.

She waited for her father to notice her. But he was turning over papers on his desk and muttering to himself. He had some crumbs in his beard and his hair stuck up in tufts.

"Father?"

He gave her a puzzled look.

Anna felt a prickle of alarm. These days her father often looked at her like that.

As if he didn't know who she was.

"Father?" she said again.

Her father's face cleared. "Anna, my dear. Max tells me you've finished all the problems I gave you. Good, good. What did you think of them?"

Anna was silent for a moment. She felt put on the spot, but she couldn't lie. "Um ... I found them rather hard."

Her father didn't look at all upset. Instead he beamed at her. "Yes, but you solved them. That's the important thing. So now you're ready to move on."

Anna's heart sank.

Her father lived for math. Sometimes she thought numbers meant more to him than she did.

But for Anna, math was like a big, black cloud hanging over her. She was tired of doing problems all the time. And sooner or later her father would find out the truth. That she was never going to be as good at math as he wanted her to be. She was never going to be able to share in his great work.

And there was another thing on her mind. It was all the fault of the secret books. They made her want something. Something she had made up her mind to ask for even if it upset her father.

Chapter 2
Gift From the Sea

Her father looked so happy with her at the moment that she almost changed her mind.

But perhaps the storm had got inside her. All that wildness beating down whatever lay in its path. Just to think of it filled her with courage.

"Father ..."

"Mmm?" Her father's eyes had drifted back to the papers on his desk. "Do you know something, Max?" he said. "I think we're going about this the wrong way. Now, if we turn the problem on its head—"

"Father," Anna said in a rush. "Can I study geography?"

He looked up, his papers forgotten. His eyes were wide with shock. But it was Max who spoke first. "What would be the point of that?" He was frowning.

Anna's heart sank. She'd hoped Max would be on her side.

"Don't you think it would be good for me?" she asked. "It would broaden my mind."

But her father shook his head. "No," he said. "No." There was panic in his voice.

Anna bit her lip. "Father, I—"

Max spoke up then. "Can't you see you're upsetting your father?"

His voice was gentle but he looked as if she'd let him down.

"I'm sorry," she said. And she meant it.

Her father looked afraid and, all of a sudden, much older. He didn't seem able to speak.

"I think you'd better go," said Max.

When she reached her room Anna saw that Biddy had been in. The jug on the table was full of hot water. Anna poured some into the china basin and washed her hands and face. Then she changed into the blue dress she wore for dinner.

She looked at the clock. It was too early to go down yet.

She crouched down in the dark corner by her chest of drawers and tugged at a loose floorboard. There, in the space under the floor, the secret books were hidden.

She pulled out the geography book and sat on her window seat to look at it. It had pictures in it of mountains and rivers. Fantastic animals— elephants and tigers. And all those people in all those countries. What harm could there be in learning more about them?

Anna shut her eyes. That way she could imagine she was a different person. Someone brave. Someone who would travel the world and see its wonders.

She opened her eyes. It was a foolish dream.

For one thing, she would have to cross the sea and she would never dare do that.

For another, she would have to speak to strangers. In her dream she could do that without fear. She enjoyed meeting them and they liked her.

In truth, she knew she would be too scared.

And it was pointless thinking about it because it was never going to happen.

Anna sighed and turned to look out of the window. Dark clouds filled the sky. The wind was still roaring, whipping up the waves.

She jumped up.

Something was bobbing about out there on the water. Something black and round.

A seal?

It didn't look like the right shape for a seal's head.

Then Anna was running down the stairs as fast as she could go. She pulled on her boots and grabbed Biddy's coat from its hook. It took both hands to open the heavy oak door and then she was outside, heading into the storm.

The path down the cliffs was steep and slippery with rain. Anna made her way down carefully, afraid of losing her balance and falling into the sea.

By the water's edge, there was a sign screwed into a rock. It said:

PRIVATE. NO LANDING.

Beside it a tall man was bent over something, his back towards her.

It was Max.

Her eyes went to the thing lying at his feet.

A tangle of dark brown hair. As brown as peat. That's what she saw first.

A face, pale as death.

A boy.

He looked about her age. Perhaps a little older. He lay stiff and still in the rain, his arms locked around a long piece of wood. Blood was seeping from his leg and staining the rocks a rusty red.

And then Anna's hand flew to her mouth. She couldn't believe her eyes.

Max was pushing the boy towards the edge of the rocks. He was going to push him into the sea!

She ran forward, shouting, "Stop!"

Max turned, startled. "Miss Anna! What are you doing here?" He stood up.

"I saw him floating in. What were you doing?"

Max shook his head. "He's dead, Miss Anna. You know your father won't want any fuss. This is the best way."

"No!" The cry of protest burst from her.

She threw herself down beside the boy, ignoring the pools of water on the rocks. "It doesn't seem right," she whispered.

She reached out her hand and touched the boy's cheek. It felt as cold as marble. Poor soul.

Max's shadow fell over them. "Go back, Miss Anna. Leave this to me."

But just then the boy's eyelids fluttered. Anna found herself staring into eyes as green as the sea.

"Oh," she breathed. "Max, look."

The boy tried to sit up, but with a groan he fell back.

"Lie still," Anna told him. She turned to Max. "Get Jasper," she said. "You'll have to carry him between you."

Max bit his lip. "But, Miss Anna," he said. "Your father—"

"I'll talk to him."

Chapter 3
I'm Real

It took Anna a while to make her father understand what had happened.

"A boy, you say? What is he doing here? Didn't he read the signs?"

"He didn't come in a boat," Anna told him. "The sea carried him here. He was drowning."

"Well, Jasper must take him to the mainland." Her father turned back to his desk as if there was nothing more to be said.

"He's hurt, Father," said Anna. "Biddy's made Jasper put him to bed. He shouldn't be moved. Isn't that right, Max?"

Max shrugged. Anna shot him a look. Why didn't he help her?

She went up to her father and put her hand on his arm. "Please don't send him away yet, Father. It would be—" She paused. "It would be cruel."

There was a long moment of silence. Anna gazed at her father, willing him to say what she wanted to hear.

Her father took her hand. Then, with a sigh, he let it fall. "I don't like it," he said. "I don't like it at all. But the boy may stay for now."

Anna breathed again.

"But, Anna," her father added. "You are to keep away from him, do you hear? Max, do you hear?"

**

At bedtime Anna pestered Biddy for news.

"His leg is broken," Biddy said. "But he doesn't seem to have any other serious injuries. He is sick. It's with being in the sea so long ... well, a body doesn't get over that so easy. It's the chill. It gets into your very bones."

Anna didn't want to hear this. She wanted the boy to get better.

The next morning she sat at her desk as usual. In front of her lay an open math book.

But she gazed out of the window. She felt too stirred up to work.

No stranger had ever set foot on the island before.

"And I'm not allowed to see him," she grumbled to herself. "He might be dying and I'm supposed to sit here doing math."

She threw down her pen and stood up.

At this time in the morning everyone was busy. Her father and Max were working up in the tower. Biddy was cooking lunch and Jasper was outside somewhere. If she just went and looked in at the boy, what harm could it do?

No one would even know.

As Anna made her way to the other side of the castle, she felt a thrill. This was an adventure. Just the sort of thing that happened in one of her secret books.

But outside the boy's room she stopped. What if he was awake? What would she say?

She peeped in. The boy was sleeping. Feeling braver, she tip-toed up to the bed.

She stood and gazed down at him.

He looked feverish and hot. He had a nasty purple bruise under one eye. But his skin was smooth and soft. It made Anna want to touch his face again.

She put out her hand, but he made a choking sound and she drew it back.

He was breathing in short gasps as if he couldn't get enough air.

"Please don't die."

Anna hadn't meant to say it out loud.

The boy opened his eyes.

She was overcome with shyness.

He kept looking at her. Today his eyes were dark, like the sea on a stormy day.

"I thought I'd dreamt you," he croaked.

Anna felt herself go red. "I'm real," she said, and felt silly.

"I can see that." He gave her a funny lop-sided smile. And then burst into a fit of choking. Anna was alarmed. She didn't know what to do.

At last he recovered and lay back on the pillows.

"You look worn out," Anna said. "You need to rest."

"What's your name?"

"Anna."

"I'm Rob. Robert Lewis."

Anna walked away but at the door she stopped to look back at him.

"You'll come again, won't you?" he asked.

"Yes," she said.

***

It was easy enough to keep her promise. She just had to make sure she chose a time when no one was around.

Rob was often asleep. If he was awake he couldn't talk much and he got tired fast so she only stayed a few minutes. But she kept going back. She couldn't help herself.

Her mind was filled with him all the time and she found it hard to think about her lessons.

One day Max said, "How are you, Miss Anna? Only you don't seem quite yourself today." He fixed her with his blue gaze.

"I'm fine, thank you." She smiled at him.

He smiled back. "I'm glad to hear it."

Max was nice. But really, compared to Rob, he did look old.

She prayed that Rob would get better. She wondered if she would be brave enough to talk to him again. She wanted to know more about him.

***

About a week later she peeped in and he was sitting up in bed.

He saw her and smiled his lop-sided smile. "Hello. I'm glad to see you. Aren't you coming in?"

Chapter 4

His Story, Her Story

Anna sat down on a chair by the bed. "I'm not supposed to be here. You haven't told Biddy I've been coming?"

Rob shook his head. "She doesn't give you much chance to say anything."

Anna laughed. The laugh was loud in the quiet house. She was surprised at how good it felt.

She looked around the room, taking it in this time. There wasn't much to see. Apart from the bed and the chair, there was only a small table with an empty glass and a jug on it. The fire was smoking. The chimney must be dirty. It was probably the first time the room had been used since they came to the castle.

She turned back to Rob. His fever must have gone. He looked more awake, clear-eyed.

"You look better."

"I'm feeling much better. And my leg is healing, I think. Jasper made a splint for it to keep it straight. Look." He pulled back the sheet to show her. From the knee down, his left leg was wrapped in a bandage. There was a piece of wood showing at the top.

"What happened?" she asked. "Were you on a ship?"

"Yes. But we ran into the storm and got blown off course. Onto some rocks. I was on deck. The mast broke and fell on my leg. But I was lucky. I managed to crawl out and dive into the sea. Nearly everyone else was down below decks." He paused. "I couldn't believe how fast the ship went down."

Anna thought about the sinking ship and all the drowned people. She shivered. "Where were you going?"

"Canada."

The name meant nothing to Anna.

"Is it a long way away?"

Rob smiled. "A very long way. But my uncle paid for my ticket. I was going to work for him. You see, my father died when I was twelve. Since then I've been helping Mother look after my younger brother and three sisters. But it's not been easy. Father didn't leave us much money. I wanted to earn some to send back to Mother."

Anna liked listening to him. It was like being told a story.

"It must be fun having a brother and sisters," she said.

Rob made a face. "Sometimes it is. But they won't always do what I tell them. They get up to all kinds of tricks, the monkeys. Apart from my oldest sister Meg. She's very nice. You'd like her."

Anna smiled but inside she felt sad. She wished she could meet Rob's family. But of course it was impossible. Her father would never let her leave the island.

"Do you miss them?" she asked.

Rob shrugged. "A little. But I'd got used to the idea that I was going away. I was looking forward to seeing the world."

Anna felt a stir of interest. "Seeing the world." It sounded just like her dream. But Rob really meant to do it.

He went on. "I wish I could let my mother know I'm safe. She'll think I drowned."

Anna thought for a moment. "I know," she said. "Next time Jasper goes to Port Finnan on the mainland he could mail a letter for you." Biddy sometimes got letters from her sister on the mainland. She read them out to Anna though she wasn't supposed to.

"What a good idea. I'll ask Biddy for some paper."

"I'd better go," Anna said. "I haven't finished today's lesson yet."

Rob looked sad.

"I'll come back soon. If I can."

***

Anna wished she could see Rob every day. But she couldn't go too often because she would get behind in her lessons. Max would be sure to notice. Several days passed before she saw him again.

"How are you?" she asked.

Rob made a face. "I want to get dressed but Biddy won't let me. I think she's afraid I'll try and walk. But I'm tired of lying here. It's boring."

Anna felt sorry for him. She would hate it if she couldn't go out.

"Tell me more about your family," she said. "I like hearing about them."

"I did all the talking last time," Rob said. "It's your turn now. I want to hear about you."

Anna was amazed. Did he mean it?

"There's not a lot to say about me."

Anna would much rather listen than talk. She wasn't used to talking. But it wasn't just that. She worried that Rob wouldn't find her very interesting.

But he kept asking questions and in the end she found herself telling him about her life on the island.

At one point Rob sat up.

"You've lived here your whole life?" He sounded astonished.

"Almost. I was born on the mainland," Anna told him. "But I can't remember anything about it. I was a baby when my father came here with me."

"What happened to your mother?"

"She died soon after I was born."

"That's so sad. You must miss her." Rob's voice was full of pity.

"Why would I miss her? I never knew her. It's not like you and your father."

A look of pain crossed his face and Anna wished she hadn't said that. She'd been right to be worried about talking. It wasn't easy. And harder with someone you didn't know. You fell into traps.

She was glad to hear a loud clang from downstairs. She jumped up. "Goodness! That's the gong. Biddy will be serving my lunch in a minute. I must go."

Chapter 5
The Number Machine

Several days passed. Anna was sorry about the way her talk with Rob had ended. Even if she dared to go to see him again, he probably wouldn't want to see her.

And she was worried about her father.

Sometimes when she went up to his room he was slumped at his table and he wouldn't speak to her. At other times he looked nervous and afraid. He didn't always make sense.

Anna was alarmed. She asked Max about it, but he told her not to worry. "We've hit a snag with his work, that's all," he told her. "Once we've figured it out, he'll be fine."

She hoped Max was right.

She couldn't help thinking of Rob and how bored he must be by now. Perhaps she should take him a book to read.

It was risky. He might give her secret away. But he seemed so nice—perhaps she could trust him.

She decided that's what she would do. Just take him a book. Not stay and talk.

***

She was surprised to find Rob out of bed. He was sitting in the chair with a blanket around him.

Anna held out the book "I wanted to give you this," she said. "To keep you from getting bored."

Rob took it from her. "Treasure Island!" He laughed. "Another island!"

"I thought you'd like it. It's about a boy who goes to sea to look for pirate treasure."

"Thank you. I'll enjoy that."

He was acting as if nothing bad had happened between them. In fact he seemed pleased to see her.

Anna thought it would be all right to stay. Just for a few minutes. She sat on the bed.

"There's just one thing," she said. "You must hide the book if anyone comes."

Rob looked puzzled.

Anna told him about the books Max left for her. "I think he tells Jasper to get them for me when he goes to Port Finnan. I'm not supposed to have them."

"Why not?"

Anna frowned. It was so hard to explain. "My father doesn't want me to find out about the world."

Rob opened his eyes wide.

"I know it must sound strange. But he's afraid that if I learn about the world, I'll want to leave the island and see it for myself. He wants me to stay here. Where it's safe."

"Safe?"

Anna nodded. "Yes, from other people. My father says they're cruel. It's better to stay away from them. That's why I'm not supposed to see you."

Rob snorted. "But that's nonsense! I think it's your father who's cruel. To keep you trapped here like a prisoner. He must be crazy."

Anna was shocked. How dare Rob say that about her father! She stood up and said in a cold voice, "You've no right to say that. You don't understand at all."

She stormed out of the room. Rob called after her but she didn't look back.

She felt angry and upset. What Rob had said was horrible. She wouldn't talk to him again.

***

After a day or two Anna was calm again. Perhaps she'd got angry over nothing. She thought about what Rob had said. Her father's ideas had always seemed normal to her. But then she didn't know anything else. Perhaps she'd been unfair to Rob. And she was missing their talks. She decided to go and see him again.

When Rob saw her his face lit up.

"You've come back! I was so afraid you wouldn't. Listen. I'm sorry for what I said. Do you forgive me?"

She could see that he meant it. "I'm sorry, too. I said too much."

She sat on the bed.

Rob was in a chair by the window, in a patch of sunshine. He was dressed today. He had on his own shirt and pants and a jacket that was too big for him. It looked like one of Jasper's.

He said, "It can't be much fun for you here. All I can see out of this window are rocks and grass. It looks very dull."

Anna protested, "It's not dull. It's beautiful! Especially now it's spring. I wish I could show you."

"I wish you could too. I'd love to go out." His face became grave. "I've been thinking about what you said. Do you think your father's right?"

Anna didn't reply for a moment. Then she said, "I used to, but now I'm not so sure." She looked at Rob. "It's because of the secret books.

In stories some people do bad things. But other people are kind and loving." She sighed. "It's very confusing."

Rob said, "I think most people are decent and try to do their best. Your father's ideas seem ... rather odd."

"He has good reason to feel as he does."

She wondered if she should be saying this. But she wanted Rob to understand.

"My father is a genius at math. He used to be at Oxford University. He invented a special machine. Max helped him. It was one that would add up numbers much faster than a human being could."

"Did he?" Rob looked impressed.

"Yes. But someone else stole his idea—a man called John Hunter. When Father said it was his idea, people mocked him. He had to leave the university. It was in the newspapers. And then my mother died."

"That must have been awful for him."

"It was. It broke his heart. That's why he came to live on the island. But he hasn't given up. He's working on a new machine, even better than the old one. Max is helping him. He says—"

Something clattered outside in the hallway. They both froze.

Anna put her finger to her lips and Rob nodded. She crept to the door and peered out.

Jasper was bent down at the end of the hallway, picking up some peat. He must have been bringing it for Rob's fire and dropped his bucket.

Thank goodness he had his back to her.

Anna gave Rob a wave. Then she fled the other way.

Chapter 6
Forget-me-not

Anna ran into her room, shaken. Jasper had so nearly found them!

"Miss Anna." The voice behind her made her jump. Max was at the door.

"Your father thought you might like to try these math problems," Max said. He held out a sheet of paper, then peered at Anna. "Are you all right? You look flushed."

His blue eyes seemed to bore into her.

"I—I'm fine. Thank you, Max."

She closed the door and leant against it.

If Max had come a minute earlier, he would have seen her room was empty. He would have looked for her and found her in Rob's room. He would have gone to her father. Rob would have been packed off to the mainland.

Thank goodness Jasper had come when he did.

What a stroke of luck.

***

For a while Anna didn't dare go to see Rob again.

But she thought about him all the time. She wondered if he was missing her.

Then one morning Max surprised her.

"Tomorrow Jasper and I are going to Port Finnan. I have matters to see to so we'll be away for the night. I'll leave you some extra work. You'll be all right, won't you?"

"Oh, yes." Anna kept her face grave.

But inside she was smiling. A whole day without Max around. She wouldn't be wasting it on math!

***

Jasper and Max left early in the morning to catch the tide. Anna was giddy with joy. As soon as Biddy went into the kitchen and shut the door, she rushed upstairs.

She burst in then stopped, surprised. Rob wasn't in the bed or the chair. With the help of a pair of crutches he was standing up!

He waved one at her. "Look! I got the idea from that book you gave me, *Treasure Island*. You know, Long John Silver the pirate only has one leg and he can get around. Jasper made these for me."

He walked a little way to show her. Anna clapped.

Rob shot her a look. "I've been walking a little bit every day. But you haven't been to see me in forever."

"No, I'm sorry. I got a scare the day that Jasper almost found us. But did you know Max and Jasper have gone to the mainland?"

"Yes. I've written a letter to my mother. Jasper is going to mail it."

Anna looked at Rob's crutches.

"It's a beautiful day and Father and Biddy are busy. Do you want to go out?"

***

It was tricky for Rob to get down the stairs, but with Anna's help he managed it. Not too far from the castle, they found a good spot to sit. It was behind some rocks so no one would be able to see them.

"Gosh, it's bright!" Rob shut his eyes and turned his face up to the light.

Below them the sea sparkled in the spring sunshine. The cliffs were a carpet of pink and blue flowers.

Anna relaxed. It was nice to sit here like this. Nice not to worry about anyone finding them together. And she was glad Rob wasn't trapped inside any more.

Rob opened his eyes.

"It's wonderful."

"I told you so," said Anna.

Anna watched the birds swoop over their heads. They filled the air with their harsh cries.

"They're noisy, aren't they?" Rob said.

"Yes," Anna said. "But I like to hear them. And watch them fly. I like the sea swallows best."

"Which are they?"

"There, look." She pointed. "Those ones with the black heads and the long tails. They have such grace. And there's something about their call. I love it."

"I can see why. They're so free, aren't they? And that wild song. It makes you shiver."

Anna felt a rush of joy. No one else had ever said that. Rob thought just the same as she did.

She couldn't help but smile at him. And he smiled back, his lop-sided, charming smile.

And then he said, "The sea swallows remind me of you. You have that grace, too."

Anna felt as if her face was on fire. She had to look away.

"You're not like any other girl I've ever met," he said. "I'll never forget you. Here." He plucked a little blue flower, a forget-me-not, and held it out to her. "So you won't forget me either."

Anna took the flower. She felt all mixed up, both happy and sad. The flower meant he liked her. But it also meant he was about to go away.

"Has Max seen your crutches?" she asked.

"Not yet. Why?"

"It doesn't matter." She didn't want to tell him. As soon as Max knew Rob could walk, he'd tell her father and he'd send Rob away.

"What do you think of Max?" Rob asked.

"He's very nice. Why?"

"I don't know. There's something about him I don't like."

"Oh, don't say that. He's been so kind to us. We'd never have managed here without him."

Rob shrugged. "Oh well, you know him better than I do."

They were silent for a moment and then Rob said, "You know, I think I understand why your father feels the way he does. Why he wants to stay away from the world. And I can see now why you're happy here. But listen, Anna. One day you may want to leave the island." He felt in his jacket pocket. "Take this in case you ever need it."

He pushed a folded piece of paper into her hand. Anna looked at it. "What is it?"

"It's my mother's address. If you want to find me, she'll know where I am."

Anna's eyes filled with tears. He wanted to see her again.

It would never happen, of course. Her father would never allow it. But it was something to hold on to. A special secret.

Chapter 7
A Terrible Day

Anna couldn't wait to see Rob again. But the next time she went to his room he wasn't there.

Of course now he could walk with the crutches he could be anywhere. Downstairs with Biddy. Or outside.

But Anna was puzzled. And hurt. He knew the time she usually came. Why wasn't he there?

A whole week went by. At last Anna had had enough. She left a note hidden in his nightshirt.

I'll come tomorrow morning.
Ten o'clock.
Please be here.

Anna

***

The next day Anna stood outside Rob's door. She held her breath and opened the door. He was there. Looking out of the window. Relief washed over her and she ran up to him.

"Rob!"

He turned. Anna froze at the grim look on his face.

What was he going to say?

But he didn't say anything. He threw his arms around her and held her tight. Anna found herself hugging him back. She didn't want it to stop.

After a while Rob let go. "Sorry," he said. "I shouldn't have done that."

"I'm glad you did."

He looked into her eyes. His face was sad.

"What is it?" she asked. "What's happened?"

"Your father has been to see me. He says I must leave."

Anna gasped. She'd known this would happen. But it was still a shock.

"When?" she whispered.

"Today."

Anna's heart dropped like a stone.

"I wanted to see you every day," Rob told her. "But when Max saw me on crutches he told me I had to help Biddy. But listen, Anna. I have something to tell you. About Max."

The tone of his voice sent a chill through her.

"What is it?"

"Yesterday I went down to the kitchen to help Biddy. She wasn't there. But Max was. I saw him put something into the fire."

"So? We always burn our trash. We don't want it to spoil the island."

"But when Max saw me he looked shifty," Rob said. "It was as if he didn't want me to see what he was doing. After he'd gone I looked in the fireplace and I found this."

He took something from his pocket and passed it to her.

It was a small piece of paper, burned brown at the edges. Anna could just about make out the words:

... could be worth a lot to me. And to you. I will be very happy to meet you. Let me know when ...

She looked at Rob. "This isn't Max's writing."

"No. Someone has written this to him. I asked Jasper about it. He said he sometimes takes letters for Max to the Post Office at Port Finnan. And picks up replies."

Anna was puzzled. "But who would Max write to? He never says anything about anyone."

"I don't know," Rob said. "But Jasper told me something else. You know they went to the mainland the other day? They were staying at an inn. But Max sent Jasper away for an hour or so. I think he was meeting the person who wrote this letter."

"Why would he do that?"

"Remember what you told me? That someone stole your father's idea and gave it to John Hunter? I think it was Max. He stole your father's work and sold it."

"What! Max wouldn't do that. He's my father's friend."

Rob shook his head. "I don't think so. I think he pretends to be. But he's not. And I think he's still stealing work from your father."

"How dare you say that?" Anna was shaking.

"I'm sorry, Anna," Rob said. "I don't want to upset you. But I'm worried about you. And your father. I think you should keep an eye on Max. You shouldn't trust him."

Anna shook her head. "You're wrong. I told you Max is good to us."

"There's something else. Something I haven't told you."

Anna didn't want to hear any more, but she had to. "What?"

"Remember the day I came, the day I nearly drowned? Well, before you arrived I spoke to Max. I said, 'Help me, please.' But he still tried to push me back into the sea."

"No." Anna stared at him, her eyes wide. It wasn't true. It couldn't be true. "Max wouldn't do that."

"But he did. He knew I was still alive. He doesn't want anyone to come here and find out what he's doing. He tried to kill me."

Anna put her hands over her ears. "Stop it! That's an awful, awful thing to say."

She burst into tears and ran from the room.

***

Anna flung herself onto her bed and sobbed her heart out.

Rob was horrible.

And he was going away and she was never going to see him again.

At long last she calmed down.

She felt worn out, numb. She just wanted to lie there but she wasn't comfortable. There was something lumpy under her pillow.

She pulled it out. It was another book. The title was printed on its green cover in gold letters. *The Moonstone*. Anna traced the letters with her finger. It sounded romantic. Just the sort of book she liked.

Max must have bought it for her in Port Finnan.

Dear Max. He was so kind to her.

He couldn't have done those terrible things. Could he?

Chapter 8
Spying

Anna had never felt more miserable. Her thoughts went round and round.

Who should she trust—Max or Rob?

She had to decide once and for all.

What would her father say?

Rob was the stranger. He had burst in and upset everything.

On the other hand, she'd known Max forever. He'd given up his life to help Anna and her father.

She must trust Max. Of course she must.

Rob would go away. And everything would go on just as it had before he came.

***

Anna got out her math books and tried to continue with her work as usual. Then she heard a voice outside.

She looked out of the window. Biddy was down in the yard talking to Jasper. Then Rob came out.

Anna's heart turned over at the sight of him.

Biddy hugged Rob. He and Jasper left the yard, turned down the path and walked behind the wall and out of sight.

Anna didn't stop to think.

She ran down the stairs, out of the door and along the path. She watched from behind a rock. She saw Jasper help Rob into the boat. Then he climbed in himself and took the oars. Anna wished Rob would look up, to see her standing there.

But he didn't.

She watched as Jasper rowed the boat away. She felt as if her heart was being carried off with them. She watched until the boat was a tiny speck on the sea. Then it vanished.

Anna turned to go back. And froze.

Max was standing further along the path. He must have been watching the boat too. He couldn't see Anna, but Anna could see his face very clearly. His lips were curved in a thin smile.

***

After Max had gone, Anna went back to the castle.

She felt very sad. But her mind was turning over and over.

Why was Max happy to see Rob go? Why did it matter to him?

Unless ...

Unless Rob was right.

Perhaps Max was happy because Rob was no longer there to spy on him.

But Anna was. She would spy on Max. She would try to find out if Rob was right after all.

The next morning Anna saw Biddy and Jasper out in the yard. One of the cows was having a calf. Anna went down to the kitchen and waited to see if anything would happen.

Before long the door opened and Max came in with some papers in his hand.

When he saw Anna he hid the papers behind his back.

"Miss Anna! What are you doing here?" He sounded angry.

"I was looking for Biddy."

"Well, you can see she's not here. You'll have to come back later."

As Anna went out of the kitchen she left the door open a crack. She peered back in. She saw Max hurry over and put the papers into the fire.

So Rob was right about that. But why was Max burning papers? Papers he didn't want her to see?

***

Anna wondered what else she could do. That afternoon when she went to see her father he was in a terrible state. He mumbled and muttered to himself. It was hard not to glare at Max, but she managed not to.

She decided to go and search Max's bedroom. She knew he was upstairs with her father, but still she felt nervous.

She took a deep breath and pushed open the door. This was the first time she'd ever been in here. She had no clear idea of what she was looking for, but what she saw in front of her made her stop dead.

Piles of clothes lay on the bed and a large leather bag sat open on the floor.

It looked as if Max was packing. As if he was going away!

Anna went over to the desk and opened a drawer. It was empty. She tried the other drawers. They were empty too.

Max must have burned all the papers he didn't want anyone to see.

She looked in the bag. There was just a box in the bottom.

Anna took the box out and looked inside. Paper, envelopes, pens … and a letter.

She picked it up. The name at the bottom of the page jumped out at her.

John Hunter, her father's rival!

She read the letter as fast as she could. John Hunter was saying thank you to Max for all his help over the years. And then came the words that made Anna's heart pound:

I have thought about what you said when we met. It is a pity the old man is no use any more. But I've looked at what he has done so far and I think we can work out the rest for ourselves. It is time for you to join me, my friend. If things go well, we shall be rich.

Chapter 9
An Enemy

Now she knew the truth for sure. Rob had been right. Max was stealing ideas from her father and selling them to his rival, John Hunter.

Jasper must have picked up the letter from the Post Office when he took Rob to Port Finnan. And now Max was planning to leave them and go and work for John Hunter.

Anna felt sick.

How could Max do this to her father?

The letter had said, "The old man is no use any more."

What a terrible thing to say.

She heard brisk footsteps in the hallway outside. Her spine turned to ice.

Max was on his way!

In a panic she slipped the letter into her pocket. She thrust the box into the bag and rushed towards the door.

Too late!

Max stood in the door. He seemed taller than ever.

"Miss Anna." Max's voice was cold. "Did you want something?"

Anna was trembling. But she faced him bravely. She could be cold too.

"I wanted to know what was going on."

"Going on?" He smiled but she could tell he was nervous. "What do you mean?"

Anna waved at the clothes on the bed. "You're going away."

"Yes."

"Have you told my father?" She was sure he hadn't.

"No. I didn't think there was any point in upsetting him."

"Did you think he wouldn't notice?" Anna could feel her anger rising. "It will crush him. Don't you care?"

Max shrugged.

"Why are you doing this?" Anna knew the answer but she wanted to hear what he had to say.

"It's simple. I've had enough of this island life. The long dark winters. The boredom."

"Why did you wait till now? You could have gone years ago." She knew why, of course. He wanted to steal as much of her father's work as he could.

"I was waiting for you."

Anna was startled. "For me? I don't understand. What do you mean?"

"I was waiting for you to grow up." Max came closer. "I want to take you away from here. This is no life for you. You should have nice clothes, books, music. You should travel and see the world. And you shouldn't be alone so much. You should have company. Haven't you ever wished for those things?"

Anna was amazed. He knew her secret thoughts! "Yes, I have," she said. "And I've been glad of the books. Thank you."

"Books?" Max looked puzzled. "What books?"

Anna blinked. He didn't know about the books! So who had been putting them secretly in her room?

But she didn't have time to think about that now. Max's blue eyes were looking deep into hers.

"Anna, my dear." Max's voice was like honey. "I could give you everything you wished for. I want to make you happy."

Just for a moment she was tempted. Some of her old feelings for Max were stirred up. And perhaps he meant what he said. Perhaps he did care for her. But then she remembered what he'd done.

The spell broke.

"I would never leave my father. And I would never ever go with you." She spat the words out. "I know what you've done."

A cold look came into Max's eyes. He took a step back. "I don't know what you mean."

"Yes, you do. You stole my father's work. It's your fault we're here. You've ruined his life. And mine. I hate you. And I'll go to the police and tell them what you and John Hunter have done."

She'd had no idea she was going to say that. But as the words flew out of her mouth she thought, *of course. That's what I must do.*

Max laughed. A horrible, mocking laugh. "You silly child! What nonsense! The police will never believe you. You have no proof."

Anna thought of the letter in her pocket and smiled to herself.

"Even if you did have proof, it would be no use," Max said. "Once I've gone tomorrow, you won't be able to leave the island." He smiled. "Are you sure you won't change your mind? Are you sure you won't come with me?"

As the meaning of his words sank in, Anna stared at him in horror.

There was only one boat on the island. Max planned to take Jasper with him. Anna and Biddy and her father would be trapped.

***

Anna ran from the room. She didn't know what to do or where to go.

Should she tell Biddy? No, Biddy would never believe her. And even if she did, it wouldn't make any difference. She wouldn't be able to stop Max.

Think, Anna, think!

And then it came to her. There was only one thing to do.

She ran up the spiral stairs to her father's room. She burst in without knocking.

Her father, startled, dropped the ink bottle he was holding. A stream of black ink spread over his papers.

"Look what you've done!" he said. "All my work ruined." He dabbed at the papers with his sleeve.

Anna pulled at his arm. "Leave it, Father. It doesn't matter."

He turned on her. "Not matter?" And then his face changed. "Who are you?" he asked.

Anna gasped. She felt as if someone had stuck a knife in her chest. "Father, it's me, Anna. Listen. We have to leave the island. We have to go away."

"Go away?" Her father's face crumpled with terror. "No! No, no, no!" Slowly he backed into the corner of the room. Then he curled up on the floor with his arms over his head.

Anna stared at him in despair. It was impossible. She couldn't get him down the stairs, let alone into the boat.

There was nothing she could do. She would have to go alone.

Chapter 10
A Friend

Anna didn't sleep that night. She lay awake and stared out of the window at the stars. They looked like tiny pin-pricks of light in the dark sky.

She felt heart-sick with sadness for her father. And her stomach churned with fear.

But she had to do it.

She had to stop Max. And she had to make sure her father got the credit for his work. She had to clear his name. Even if it was too late for him to know it.

By dawn Anna was up and dressed.

In her pocket she had some money she'd taken from her father's cash box, and the letter from John Hunter.

She crept downstairs. As she passed the kitchen she saw Jasper's gun leaning against the wall. She stopped.

Her plan had seemed simple. She would row to the mainland. Somehow she would find her way to the police and tell them what had happened. They would come back to the island and arrest Max. She would find a doctor. He would help her have her father taken somewhere where he could be looked after.

It all made perfect sense.

But Anna had never rowed a boat before and she was afraid of drowning.

And for her plan to work she would have to speak to total strangers. What if they turned out to be as horrible as her father said?

She'd never fired a gun. But it seemed like it might be a good idea to have one now.

She picked it up and took it with her.

***

The boat was half way up the beach. Anna wondered if she would be strong enough to push it into the water. First she had to lift out the stones Jasper had put in it to stop it blowing away.

She was reaching for the last one when she heard footsteps crunch over the pebbles.

She spun around.

It was Jasper!

Anna grabbed the gun and pointed it at him.

"Don't come any nearer. If you do, I'll shoot."

Jasper stayed where he was. He didn't say anything.

Anna was trembling, but she said, "I know all about you and Max. I'm taking the boat. You won't stop me."

"I've not come to stop you. I've come to help you." Jasper's voice was soft. "And you've got it wrong, Miss Anna. I'm not Mr. Maxwell's friend."

Anna stared at him. Was he trying to trick her?

"Listen, Miss Anna. I've thought for a long time that Mr. Maxwell was up to something. But I didn't know what. It was your friend Rob who tipped me off."

Anna was startled. Rob had told Jasper?

"Then I heard the pair of you last night. So I knew Mr. Maxwell was going to take the boat today. I heard the door this morning and thought it might be him. I came to stop him, but then I saw it was you. And I thought you could use some help."

Anna's mind was racing. "What makes you think Rob was my friend?"

Jasper nodded. "I knew you were seeing a lot of him."

Anna stared at him. And it all fell into place.

Jasper knew she was seeing Rob and he hadn't told anyone.

Then there was the day Max would have caught her if Jasper hadn't dropped the peat.

And there was something else.

"The books," she said. "That was you, wasn't it? You bought those books for me when you went to Port Finnan."

Jasper nodded. He looked shy. "I hope they were all right. I'm not much of a reader."

Anna put down the gun. "They were perfect. Thank you."

What a fool she'd been. All along Jasper had been her friend.

Jasper nodded again. "Miss Anna, I think you'd better get a move on or it'll be too late."

She looked at the sea. It was calm this morning, shining like silk.

"Do you want me to go?" Jasper asked.

Anna turned to face him and her chin went up. "No. It's right that I should go. For my father's sake. It's better for you to stay and keep an eye on Max."

"I will, don't you fear."

Jasper told her what to do when she reached Port Finnan and how to find the police station. He gave her a shy smile. "I don't think you'll need a gun there, Miss Anna."

Anna blushed and handed it over.

Jasper helped her into the boat. He showed her what to do with the oars and then he pushed the boat into the water.

"You'll be fine, Miss Anna. Just remember, look at the boat, not at the sea. And keep your back to the sun. You'll come to two black rocks sticking up out of the water. Go between them and you'll see where to land."

Anna tried to row. She splashed a lot and the boat stayed where it was.

"Dig deeper into the water with the oars," Jasper called.

She tried again and the boat began to move away from the beach.

Jasper's voice came over the water. "God speed, Miss Anna. And don't worry about your father. I'll look after him."

***

At first Anna found it hard to stop the boat zig-zagging. But then she began to pull on both oars at the same time and started moving in a straight line.

As she moved further from the island, she became aware of the sea on all sides of her.

Just once she looked at it and her stomach lurched with terror.

She remembered what Jasper had said. She looked down at the wooden boards of the boat and after a while she felt better.

The sun was warm on her back. The boat glided along. Sea swallows flew overhead as if they were travelling with her. The air was full of their wild song.

She thought about what lay ahead. Once Max was dealt with, she would make sure her father was safe and comfortable.

And then she would go and find Rob.

More from *Stoke Books* ...

Text Game
KATE CANN

Mel's so excited – she has a new boyfriend and he's perfect. She can't believe he's going out with her.

But then the weird texts start. They say Ben's cheating on her, seeing someone else.

Should Mel ignore them? Or could they be telling the truth?

Them
L. A. WEATHERLY

They are the most popular girls in school.

If you're in, you're cool. If you're out, you're nobody.

How far would you go to get in with **Them**?

One unlucky boy is about to find out ...

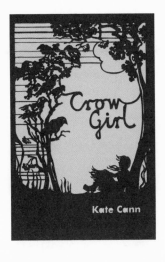

Crow Girl
KATE CANN

"She changed like Spiderman,"

"Yeah! Bird Girl!"

"No. Crow Girl..."

Lily Stanfield is an outsider. Girls bully her, boys don't notice she's alive. But when she meets the crows in the Wakeless Woods, a new Lily is born...

Ghosting
KEITH GRAY

Nat's sister Sandy speaks to the dead. It's a gift. And a good way to make a living.

Only thing is, it isn't true.

So imagine Nat and Sandy's surprise when the dead start to speak back. But it seems the dead are the least of their problems...

www.stokebooks.com

1921